The Knights of Fix-a-Lot

adapted by
Iona Treahy

based on the
teleplay by
**Sarah Ball and
Jimmy Hibbert**

SIMON SPOTLIGHT
An imprint of Simon & Schuster Children's Publishing Division
1230 Avenue of the Americas, New York, New York 10020
Text and design © 2003 BBC Worldwide Ltd.
© 2003 HIT Entertainment PLC and Keith Chapman.
Previously published in 2003 by BBC Worldwide Ltd.
First American edition, 2004
SIMON SPOTLIGHT and colophon are registered trademarks of Simon & Schuster.
Manufactured in the United States of America   First Edition   10 9 8 7 6 5 4 3 2 1
ISBN 0-689-86288-1

One morning someone arrived at Bob's yard. His name was Bob too. "Hi, Dad," said Bob. "I didn't expect you until the summer."

"I was bored at home," explained Bob's dad. "I need a project."

Just then the phone rang. Bob's dad answered it.

"Hello, this is Dr. Mountfitchet," said the voice on the phone. "A castle needs fixing. Can you help?"

"Yes, I can!" said Bob's dad. Now he had something to do!

Dr. Mountfitchet came to Bob's yard and showed Bob's dad a plan of the castle. She thought he was Bob the Builder!

"Let's go over to the castle now to take a look," Bob's dad said.

There was a moat around the castle, so they couldn't go inside. "Knights—like Sir Lancelot—would lower a drawbridge over the moat to let in friends, and raise it to keep out enemies," explained Dr. Mountfitchet.

"That's your first job, team," said Bob's dad. "Build a drawbridge."

"**Can we fix a lot?**" called Scoop.

"**Yes, we can!**" said Dizzy, giggling. "Fix a lot . . . Fix-a-lot!"

"Meet the knights of Fix-a-lot!" said Muck. "Bob's dad is Sir Boss-a-lot!"

Bob's dad
decided to fix
the castle gate.
But then he got stuck!
"Help!" he yelled.
Bob's dad was stuck to
the chains that raised
and lowered the gate.
Lofty had to rescue
him with his hook.

To keep his dad out of trouble, Bob asked him to trim the maze hedges.

A few minutes later Bob's dad shouted, "Help! I'm lost in the maze!"

Lofty had to lift Bob high up so he could see his dad and tell him how to get out.

Later that day Bob was
clipping some ivy when
he found a hidden door.

"It's the lost door
to the dungeon!" cried
Dr. Mountfitchet.
They pushed it open and
went inside. But Bob's dad closed the door
by mistake and it would not open again.
They were trapped!

Bob's dad bravely went to look for a way out. He fell against a wall—and it opened! He was pushed out into the maze hedge again!

Bob's dad cut through the hedges to escape from the maze.

"Oh, no!" said Bob when he saw the hedges. "They're ruined!"

Dr. Mountfitchet thought the hedges looked wonderful. "They're shaped like knights," she said, beaming.

When the castle was
finally fixed there was
a grand opening with lots
of visitors—including Bob's mom!
Everyone had dressed up.
"Who's going to be king?"
asked Dr. Mountfitchet.
"You can be king, Dad," said Bob.
"No, you'd make a better king," insisted Bob's dad.

So Bob declared, "I, King of Fix-a-lot, knight thee. Arise, Sir Dad-a-lot!"